D1014522

JACOB TWO-TWO

on the High Seas

JACOB TWO-TWO

on the High Seas

GARY FAGAN

Illustrated by Dušan Petričić

Based on the character created by Mordecai Richler

TUNDRA BOOKS

Published in Canada by Tundra Books
75 Sherbourne Street, Toronto, Ontario M5A 2P9

Published in the United States by Tundra Books of Northern New York,
P.O. Box 1030, Plattsburgh, New York 12901

Library of Congress Catalogue Number: 2008911580

LIBRARY AND ARCHIVES CANADA CATALOGUING IN PUBLICATION

Fagan, Cary
Jacob Two-Two on the high seas / Cary Fagan;
illustrated by Dušan Petričić.

ISBN 978-0-88776-895-8

I. Petričić, Dušan II. Title.

PS8561.A375J32 2009   jC813'.54   C2008-908031-9

We acknowledge the financial support of the Government of Canada through the Book
Publishing Industry Development Program (BPIDP) and that of the Government of Ontario
through the Ontario Media Development Corporation's Ontario Book Initiative. We further
acknowledge the support of the Canada Council for the Arts and the Ontario Arts Council
for our publishing program.

Design: CS Richardson

Printed and bound in Canada

1 2 3 4 5 6   14 13 12 11 10 09

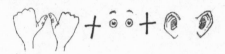

To Kathy Lowinger, in gratitude – C. F.

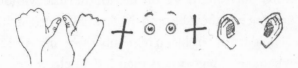

CHAPTER 1

Once there was a boy called Jacob Two-Two. He had two ears and two eyes and two arms and two feet and two shoes. He had two older sisters, Emma and Marfa, and two older brothers, Daniel and Noah. And they all lived in a rambling house on Kingston Hill, in Surrey, England.

He was called Jacob Two-Two because he was two plus two plus two years old. Also, because nobody in his family ever heard him the first time, so he had to say everything two times. Jacob Two-Two had become used to his name, but now he was beginning to worry about it.

Of course, worrying was a natural thing for Jacob Two-Two. He worried about whether he would be able to put toothpaste on his toothbrush without squeezing half the tube onto the floor. He worried that he would never be able to remember whether African elephants had bigger ears than Indian elephants, or whether it was the other way around. But worrying about his name was different. Soon, it would be Jacob Two-Two's birthday. He wouldn't be two plus two plus two years old anymore. He would be two plus two plus two . . . plus one. He was sure that his brothers and sisters, who thought it was great fun to tease him, would start to call him Jacob Two-Two *Plus One*!

He could just imagine it. "Jacob Two-Two Plus One, leave my toys alone!" Or "Jacob Two-Two Plus One, don't touch that television channel!" How awful that would be! So in order to make sure that didn't happen, Jacob decided something. He decided that he would have to get his brothers and sisters and his mother and father to forget his birthday this year. That was a pretty big sacrifice since it meant that he wouldn't get any presents. But Jacob Two-Two decided that not being stuck with that ridiculous name was worth it. The only question was *how?* He brooded and brooded, but still he couldn't come up with a plan to get his family to forget his birthday.

And then one day, exactly one month before Jacob's birthday, his father and mother gathered them all together in the living room for an announcement. "Your mother and I have made a big decision," Jacob's father said. "It is time for us to return to my home and native land."

"Where is that?" Jacob asked. "Where is that?"

His father unfurled a large map of the world. "That is this enormous pink country right here. Canada."

"*Canada?*" said Daniel with a sneer. "Canada sucks!"

"I don't want to move to Canada," said Marfa. "My friends all live here."

"Now, children, no whining," said their father. "You'll only prove to us that we've spoiled you. The decision has already been made. We're going to move to Canada and live in the city of Montreal, where I grew up. The change will make you all better children. It will give you a sense of your roots. It will allow you to play ice hockey. And it will introduce you to the sublime taste of a smoked-meat sandwich."

"Tell them the other reason why we're returning," said Jacob's mother with a smile.

His father modestly lowered his eyes. "As you children know, my new and very important book has just been published. As a result, the prime minister of Canada, Perry Pleaser, is begging me to return. The simple truth is, my country needs me."

"If that is England," Jacob said, pointing to the small country that he recognized, "and that is Canada, then what is the blue in between? What is the blue?"

"Don't you know anything?" said Emma. "That's the Atlantic Ocean."

"Do we have to swim to Canada?" asked Jacob. "Do we have to swim?" Not being a very strong swimmer was something else that worried Jacob.

"Of course not, my boy. We're going on a ship!"

"An ocean liner!" said Daniel excitedly. "Is it one of those luxury ships? Is it the *Queen Elizabeth II*?"

"I'm afraid there were no tickets available on the *Queen Elizabeth II*," said Jacob's father. "But I'm sure the ship we're going on is very nice. It's called the SS *Spring-a-Leak*. Just think, kids, five days on the

high seas. It's going to be splendid. I plan to spend the whole time sitting in a deck chair, drinking pineapple juice and reading the newspapers."

Jacob Two-Two wasn't so sure that it would be splendid, but he decided not to say anything, as his brothers and sisters would only make fun of him. The one good thing was that they would be on the ship for his birthday. Maybe, just maybe, everybody would forget about it.

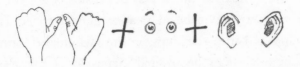

CHAPTER 2

Everything that Jacob's family owned had to be packed. Soon, the house was filled with boxes. There were boxes in the living room, boxes in the dining room, boxes in the kitchen, and boxes in all the bedrooms.

Jacob's brothers and sisters found more interesting uses for them. Daniel and Marfa used two empty flattened boxes to slide down the stairs. "Get out of the way, Jacob!" Daniel called out. "We're learning how to toboggan, like they do in Canada."

"Can I try, can I try?" Jacob asked excitedly.

"You're too little. Now move out of the way or you're going to get knocked down. Yahoo!"

Jacob had to move fast because Daniel came whooshing down the stairs at breakneck speed. He wandered into the living room, where he found none other than the intrepid Shapiro and the fearless O'Toole, otherwise known as Emma and Noah. The duo wore Day-Glo blue jeans and flying golden capes, and they had the spine-chilling *Child Power* emblem emblazoned on their chests. They were inside a large wardrobe box, hanging a flashlight from the cardboard ceiling and taping a transistor radio to the wall.

"What are you doing?" asked Jacob. "What are you doing?"

"We're building our headquarters," said the intrepid Shapiro.

"How neat. Can I come in? Can I come in?" Jacob asked.

"These headquarters are for superheroes only," said the fearless O'Toole. "Are *you* a superhero?"

Jacob had to admit that he wasn't. Head lowered, he walked slowly away – and bumped right into his mother.

"Well, young man," she said. "I can see that you

need something to do. How about you pack up your own toys?"

"I can do that, I can do that," Jacob said.

"You must pack only what you really need," his mother said. "You've got to decide what toys and games to take and what to leave behind."

Jacob hurried up to his room, glad to have a big kid's job to do. He stood among his stuffed animals, his toy cars and aeroplanes, his games and puzzles. How could he possibly decide what to take and what to leave behind? Did he need his Captain Crinkle secret decoder ring? Should he take his stuffed kangaroo with the missing eye? Jacob pondered these difficult questions. When he couldn't come up with the answers, he decided to ask his father.

So many boxes filled the house that it took Jacob a long time to even *find* his father, who was lying on the sofa in the library, reading the newspaper. When he saw Jacob, he put down the paper. "Son, perhaps I better tell you a few things about Canada," his father said.

"Tell me, tell me."

"First of all, the winter is very cold. It's so cold that everyone has to carry an ice pick. That way, if your boots become frozen to the ground, you can chip yourself free."

Jacob was astonished. "What else? What else?" he asked.

"You have to watch out for polar bears and mountain lions on the way to school. The polar bears will steal your lunch, but the mountain lions want your satchel of books. They're very eager to learn. Now, at home, before you take a bath, you may have to remove a seal from the tub, which is quite hard to do because they're so slippery. Don't try to take your bath with the seal because it will be sure to hog the soap."

Jacob was so amazed by these facts that he forgot what he had meant to ask his father. In the end, it was his mother who ended up packing his toys. A big moving van came, and two hefty men took all the boxes out of the house. When at last they were finished, all that was left were seven small suitcases, one for each of them to take on the ship.

"Good-bye, house," said Marfa.

"Farewell, England," said Daniel.

"We hope you'll be alright without us," the intrepid Shapiro and the fearless O'Toole said together.

Jacob Two-Two sniffled a little. He didn't like leaving old things behind, and he didn't like encountering new things. He felt his father's hand on his shoulder.

"Don't worry, Jacob. Everything will be fine."

"Will it? Will it?" Jacob asked too quietly for anyone to hear. A black London taxicab pulled up to take them all to the port.

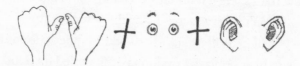

CHAPTER 3

As Jacob got out of the taxicab, he stared at the ship docked in the port. It was old and rusty and looked more like a big tugboat than a real ocean liner. The black letters spelling out the name SS *Spring-a-Leak* were chipped and faded.

"That's our ship?" Daniel said, as the taxi drove away. "It's a floating dump."

"Well, it was the only ship available," Jacob's father said. "Now come on, kids, where's your sense of adventure?"

"We forgot to pack it," Marfa said.

Jacob's parents went up the gangplank first, followed by Daniel and Marfa and Emma and Noah, and finally Jacob, pushing up his suitcase. At least, he was supposed to be pushing it up the gangplank. Mostly it appeared as though the suitcase was pushing him *down*. But at last he reached the deck, where a man in a bright, white uniform and cap stood at attention. He had blue eyes, blond hair, and an enormous dimple in his chin. His white teeth shone even brighter than his brass buttons.

"Welcome aboard!" said the man, smiling even more. "I'm Captain Sparkletooth. It's my job to make sure that you have a smooth ride all the way. Without me, this ship can't go anywhere. Yes, it takes great skill, knowledge, and courage to be the captain, not to mention good looks. It's true that I got the lowest marks in my class at naval training school, but I was voted most handsome. For those of you who care to know about our route, we will be sailing in a northeast direction."

"Excuse me, Captain," said a short man in a blue uniform. "Actually, we'll be sailing in a southwest direction."

"Yes, of course. That's what I meant. This is the

ship's first mate, Mr. Scrounger. I don't have the foggiest idea why he's called the first mate since there's no second mate, but that's how we do things on a boat."

"A *ship,* sir. We call it a ship."

"Right, a ship. Now, if you'll all go and put your suitcases into your rooms–"

"Cabins, sir."

"I mean cabins. Meanwhile, I'll go to the place where I, uh, drive the ship."

"The wheelhouse."

"What a funny name. Anyway, I'm going to go there and pull the whistle. It makes a wonderful tooting noise. Whenever I pull the whistle, the crew jumps into action, running every which way, climbing here and there. It's wonderful to see. I get a kick out of it every time. Now, I hope you will dine at my table tonight. It's a great honor to dine at the captain's table, especially when he is as deliriously handsome as I am. Which reminds me – I haven't looked at myself in a mirror for at least ten minutes. Until dinner then!"

The captain turned, took a step, and slipped on a coiled rope. It was a good thing that Mr. Scrounger was there to catch him. Jacob suspected that the first mate was used to catching the captain. Going down a winding metal staircase on the way to their cabins, Jacob heard the shrill *toot! toot!* of the whistle. Captain Sparkletooth must have really been enjoying himself.

Jacob Two-Two felt the ship slowly begin to move. They were heading out to sea!

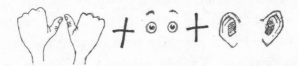

CHAPTER 4

Jacob Two-Two soon discovered that the SS *Spring-a-Leak* didn't attract just any ordinary passengers. On the deck, after unpacking his suitcase, Jacob met the Bubov Brothers, three acrobats who were on their way to join a circus. "Glad to meet you," said the eldest brother.

"*Very* glad to meet you," said the middle brother.

"*Very, very* glad to meet you," said the youngest brother.

The Bubov Brothers didn't walk along the deck. Instead, they each did a series of front handsprings, going head-over-heels. When one of them wanted to get a blanket to use on a deck chair, he simply leapt up and onto his brother's shoulders to reach it.

Also on board was Percy Swishbottom and his ventriloquist dummy, Hector. Percy wasn't a very good ventriloquist – he moved his own lips when Hector talked. "I'm still training him," Hector the Dummy said, rolling his eyes to the back of his wooden head.

Jacob was even more interested in a man who wore a white-and-blue striped jacket and a porkpie hat. The man handed Jacob a small box. Jacob was startled when out of the box sprang a rubber snake with a card in its mouth. The card said

Jethro Peabody
Toy Inventor
I might have no hair, but I'm young at heart!

"Are you really a toy inventor?" Jacob asked. "Are you?"

"I certainly am," Mr. Peabody said, doffing his hat to reveal a shiny, bald head. "Perhaps you know some of my inventions. For example, my underwater train set, my square basketball, and my exploding banjo."

"No, I don't know them," Jacob said, hoping not to hurt the inventor's feelings.

"Well, they weren't as popular as I had hoped. How about my bicycle that transforms into a dentist's chair?"

"Not that either. Not that either."

"Well, just wait and see. My next invention – as soon as I think of it – will be a big hit. Why, it'll be bigger than the hula hoop!"

But the person Jacob was most glad to meet was exactly his age and exactly his height. She had straight bangs, green eyes, and she wore a blue coat, a white hat, and shiny shoes with bows, just like a girl out of an old storybook. She came up to Jacob and said, "I'm Cynthia Francis Louise Snootcastle. But you can call me Cindy. What's your name?"

"Jacob Two-Two."

"Nice to meet you, Jacob Two-Two," she said, shaking his hand. "Is this your first time on a ship?"

"Yes it is, yes it is."

"You're lucky. The first time is most special. This is my second. We came over three months ago, so that I could have finishing lessons."

"Finishing lessons?" asked Jacob. "What are they? What are they?"

"That's where you learn which fork to eat your salad with, how to curtsy when you meet a prince or a queen, and the proper way to laugh."

"There's a proper way to laugh?" Jacob asked in surprise.

"Oh, yes. You shouldn't open your mouth too much or laugh too loudly. If you want to know the truth, finishing lessons are very boring. But you know what? I have a treasure in my pocket."

"You do? You do?"

"Uh-huh. I haven't shown it to anybody because it's a secret. But I'll show you."

Jacob was very curious to see the treasure in Cindy's pocket, but before she had a chance to show him, a woman came over and grasped Cindy by the arm. She was a big woman in a hat with peacock feathers and a fur collar on her coat.

"Cindy! Who are you talking to?"

"I'm speaking to Jacob Two-Two, Mother."

Cindy's mother looked down at Jacob. Then she turned and saw Jacob's father, a tall glass with ice in one hand, settling down into a deck chair. *"Hmmpf!* Don't tell *me* what they are. I can see very well for myself. They are upstarts. Johnny-come-latelies.

They are people who have to *work* for a living. The Snootcastles associate with a higher class of people, Cindy, a much higher class!"

CHAPTER 5

At that moment, Jacob heard the tinkling of a bell. He saw the first mate, Mr. Scrounger, standing on the deck and shaking the bell. "All right, children," he announced. "One of my duties is to make sure you kids have a good time. So this afternoon, we're going to play shuffleboard and Ping-Pong."

"I love Ping-Pong, I love Ping-Pong," said Jacob. "Oh, those games are for the big kids," said Mr. Scrounger with a glint in his eyes. "I've got something special for the smaller children."

"Come on, Marfa, Noah, and Emma. Let's head for the games room!" said Daniel.

So the big kids ran off, leaving Jacob and Cindy behind. Mr. Scrounger steered them forward. "This way, you two. Let's go and have some extra-special fun." He pushed them through a small metal door and shooed them down a winding iron staircase. They walked across the lower deck, where the sleeping cabins were, through another metal door, and down into the belly of the ship. It began to get warm. Jacob's skin felt clammy. A grinding noise grew louder and louder; thumps and clangs added to the din.

"Are you sure that children are allowed down here?" Cindy asked.

"Of course I'm sure," said Mr. Scrounger, who wasn't smiling any longer. "Are you telling me that you aren't having a grand time? Here's the last door. Look out now, there will be a blast of hot air when I open it. But it's nothing to worry about!"

Mr. Scrounger grasped the handle of the door with both hands and pushed with all his might. The door opened, and an awful, hot, sooty blast struck them all in the face. "Hurry up, I can't hold this door all day!" growled Mr. Scrounger. Jacob grimaced as he and Cindy went through the door, followed by Mr. Scrounger. The door slammed behind them.

They were in the enormous engine room. Here, great wheels turned and iron shafts chugged up and down. In the center stood the engine that ran the ship. Its door was open and giant red flames could be seen inside. Beside the engine was a mountain of shining, black coal, and standing on top of the coal was a huge man. He wore dirty trousers and a ripped T-shirt. His big face strained with effort as he threw a shovelful of coal. When the coal hit the flames, it made them roar even higher.

Mr. Scrounger put his hands around his mouth and shouted. "Morgenbesser! Come here!" But the man couldn't hear over the noise of the engine. "Morgenbesser!"

This time the huge man stopped. He turned with a frown. When he saw them, he raised his shovel and plunged it into the pile of coal, leaving it standing upright. He took one big stride after another until he reached them and came to a stop, crossing his massive arms. Jacob felt his knees shaking. Both he and Cindy took a step back.

"What is it?" the giant man said in a deep voice.

"Here are two helpers for you. Jacob Two-Two and Cindy. Put them to work – and don't go easy on them. Do you understand?"

Morgenbesser looked at the two children and smiled. "I understand," he said.

Mr. Scrounger laughed as he turned around, pulled open the door, and let himself out. Jacob and Cindy were now alone with the huge man. Jacob felt Cindy nervously take his hand. *Be brave,* Jacob told himself.

"Hello, Morgenbesser," Jacob managed to squeak out. "It's nice to meet you, nice to meet you."

Morgenbesser stared at them harder. He put his tremendous hand into his trouser pocket and brought it out again. He held out his fist and slowly opened his fingers.

"Would either of you like a piece of gum?"

Jacob looked down at Morgenbesser's open hand. In his palm rested two wrapped squares of Pinko-Winko Extra-Stretch Bubble Gum, which happened to be Jacob's favorite. He wasn't sure if he should take it, but Cindy whispered to him, "It would be most impolite to refuse." They each took a piece. The wrapper was smudged with coal dust, but inside the gum was fresh. Jacob popped it into his mouth.

"Thank you," Jacob said. "Are you going to make us shovel coal now? Are you?"

For the first time, Morgenbesser smiled. "I'm supposed to do whatever Mr. Scrounger tells me. But I don't like him very much. He isn't a nice man. No doubt he isn't putting the big kids to work because the parents would believe them if they told. He thinks they won't believe you. But I would enjoy just having your company. It gets awfully lonely down here by myself. You don't happen to like playing checkers, do you?"

"I do like checkers. I do," Jacob said.

"So do I. And I'm really good," said Cindy.

"Then follow me." Morgenbesser led them to the other side of the engine room. There was a small table made from wooden boards, with three barrels placed around it. Morgenbesser had used a piece of coal to draw a checkerboard on top of the table. He used pennies and nickels for playing pieces. The three of them took turns playing the game. Cindy *really* was good. She beat Morgenbesser eight times and Jacob five times. Jacob beat Cindy twice and Morgenbesser four times, so he didn't mind. While they were playing, Jacob noticed a ring on Morgenbesser's finger. On the ring were the letters WWWL. Jacob knew what those letters stood for – the Wacky World Wrestling League.

"Were you a wrestler? Were you a wrestler?" Jacob asked excitedly.

"Yes, I was," Morgenbesser said. "But I didn't like throwing people up in the air and slamming them and stomping on them. So I had to quit."

"Do you know The Hooded Fang? Do you know him?"

"Sure I do. He's a very sweet guy, although he doesn't like it if you try to get mushy. We had two wrestling matches. He won the first and I won the second, so we tied. Oh, goody, I can jump three of your pieces!"

Morgenbesser told Jacob and Cindy that they shouldn't trust Mr. Scrounger. Lately, the first mate seemed to be up to even more no-good than usual. He advised them to keep an eye out for anything odd. "If you see anything suspicious, come and tell Morgenbesser," said their new friend.

"We will, we will," Jacob said. And because he liked Morgenbesser so much, he let him win the next game.

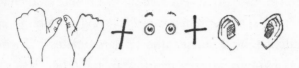

CHAPTER 6

Just before it was time for dinner, Morgenbesser smeared coal dust on Jacob's and Cindy's hands and faces. When Mr. Scrounger returned, he found them busily shoveling coal into a wheelbarrow. "Well, Morgenbesser, I can see these two have had some real sailor's experience! Now come along, you two, and get washed up. We can't have your parents see you like this."

When Jacob and Cindy entered the dining room, there wasn't a smudge of coal dust on them. Mr. Scrounger had made sure they scrubbed their hands and faces with harsh soap. Jacob was glad to return to his family, and he couldn't wait to tell them about how mean Mr. Scrounger was. The dining room was enormous, with a high ceiling and real crystal chandeliers, and an orchestra was playing a waltz. Jacob watched the Bubov Brothers balance plates and wine glasses on their noses to entertain the other guests at their table. He listened to Percy Swishbottom argue with his dummy over who should get the maraschino cherry in their drink. He observed Mr. Peabody demonstrate a ukulele that squirted water when it was strummed.

Jacob's family sat at the captain's table. So was Cindy's mother, who immediately called her over. "Cynthia Francis Louise Snootcastle, you come right here. Sit down at once. It shows ill breeding to be late. I expect such behavior from your little friend here, but not from you. As you can see, we have been seated with your new friend's family. If I had known, I would not have pleaded for seats at the captain's table."

Jacob sat down between his parents. "There you are, Jacob," his father said. "Having such a good time that you forgot what time it was, I suppose."

"Yes, you must have been having fun," Captain

Sparkletooth said. "You and Cindy are the only children who did not have their photographs taken with me. Everyone considers a photograph with me to be the most precious souvenir of the voyage. But don't be disappointed, we can take them tomorrow."

"But I only had fun because of Morgenbesser. Because of Morgenbesser!" Jacob said. "Mr. Scrounger wanted Cindy and me to work in the engine room."

"The engine room?" Captain Sparkletooth said. "That's a dangerous place. Children are not permitted there. *I'm* not permitted there. You must have a very good imagination, Jacob Two-Two."

"But Jacob didn't imagine it," Cindy said. "I was there too."

"Child, it is rude to be so insistent," said Mrs. Snootcastle. "No doubt it is the influence of that boy."

"Why don't we ask Mr. Scrounger?" suggested Captain Sparkletooth.

Mr. Scrounger was making sure that the underpaid waiters did not slip any food into their pockets. He came over and saluted.

"Yes, Captain?"

"Could you tell us what Jacob Two-Two and Cindy did this afternoon?"

"Most certainly. We all played a game. Jacob Two-Two called it Engine Room. We pretended that sugar cubes were pieces of coal. It was jolly good fun."

Jacob saw that Morgenbesser was right. Mr. Scrounger had chosen Jacob and Cindy because he knew that the grown-ups wouldn't believe them. He gave up trying to tell the truth.

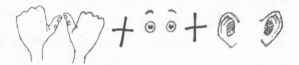

CHAPTER 7

That night, Jacob slept on a ship for the first time. He had a lower berth, which was a kind of bunk that folded out from the wall, with Noah above him and Daniel across from him. The only glow was moonlight coming in from the cabin's oval window. His older brothers had been reading, but soon the gentle rocking of the ship had put them to sleep.

But Jacob was still awake. He thought about his new friends, Cindy and Morgenbesser, and how glad he was to have met them. He worried about what Mr. Scrounger might be up to. Worrying about Mr. Scrounger wasn't the same as worrying about tying his shoes so that the laces didn't always come un-done, nor was it like worrying about buttoning his shirt properly. It was a bigger worry than that. But what *was* Mr. Scrounger up to?

Jacob tried to put himself to sleep by counting by twos. "Two . . . four . . . six," he whispered. But it didn't help. Then he heard something.

A knock. There it was again, on the door of their cabin. He crept out of bed and over to the door and whispered, "Who is it? Who is it?"

"It's Cindy. I need to talk to you."

Jacob opened the door. There she was, in her pajamas too. "Come with me," she said. Jacob closed the door gently behind him. He and Cindy crept down the hall and stopped in front of her cabin door. "I heard a strange fluttering noise. Then I heard a squawking noise," said Cindy.

"What was it? What was it?" asked Jacob, becoming even more worried.

"I don't know, but I think we should find out. It went somewhere down the hall. Let's follow it."

"But I'm not supposed to wander around the ship at night. I'm not supposed to," Jacob said.

Cindy looked at him impatiently. "Fine. Wait for

me in my room. I'll come back and report what I find."

"But isn't your mother in there?"

"She's sound asleep. Don't worry, go in. I'll be back in a minute."

Cindy opened her door and pushed Jacob inside. The room was dark. Mrs. Snootcastle must have pulled the curtain across the window. After a moment, he could see the little sink, table, the berths, and the mound that was Mrs. Snootcastle, under her blanket. Mrs. Snootcastle was snoring. It sounded like somebody sawing through a drainpipe. Suddenly, Mrs. Snootcastle coughed, snorted, and turned over.

"Cindy? Ah . . . Cindy?" she muttered.

What was he to do? Jacob tried to make his voice sound like Cindy's. "I'm here, Mother," he said.

Mrs. Snootcastle snorted again, as if she were not really awake. "Did you . . . did you remember to kiss the garbage and take your father out to the curb?" she asked.

"Yes, Mother."

"Good. . . ." Mrs. Snootcastle's voice faded away, and she started to snore again.

A moment later, the door opened and Cindy pulled Jacob back into the hallway. "Your mother almost woke up. She almost woke up," Jacob said.

But Cindy ignored him. "I found it! I found what the fluttering was!" she said.

"What was it? What was it?" Jacob asked.

"It's down at the end of the hall. Want to come and see it?"

Of course Jacob did. He and Cindy took off down the hall. As they turned around the corner, he saw something on the deck, something green and yellow. It was a bird. Not just a bird, but a parrot! The bird turned its head to look at them, stretched out its wings, and said in a squawking voice, *"I'm in love with a vacuum cleaner! I'm in love with a vacuum cleaner!"*

Jacob and Cindy looked at each other and giggled. The parrot could talk, and it said things twice, just like Jacob Two-Two. Jacob crouched down and in a gentle voice, said, "Come here, little parrot, I won't hurt you. I won't hurt you."

"Mashed potatoes on your head! Mashed potatoes on your head!" squawked the parrot. Jacob and Cindy giggled again, but just then, one of the cabin doors opened and out came Mr. Scrounger. He wasn't dressed in his uniform, instead he wore a nightgown, with a floppy nightcap on his head.

"So there you are, you pesky bird," Mr. Scrounger said.

"Is he your parrot?" asked Cindy.

"Yes, he is. I've been teaching him to talk. But he won't say the things I want him to say, the things that parrots are supposed to say, like 'Polly want a cracker' and 'Pieces of eight.' It's very disappointing, especially since I don't even like birds. Now come on, bird, get back in here."

"Kiss my feathered butt! Kiss my feathered butt!" said the parrot.

"Why, you . . ." muttered Mr. Scrounger. He lunged for the bird, but it fluttered up into the air, and Mr. Scrounger landed facedown on the deck. Then the bird flew through the open cabin door. Mr. Scrounger got up, straightening his nightgown and cap. "There will be no crackers for you," he said, as he walked into his cabin and slammed the door behind him. Jacob and Cindy said good night and went back to their own cabins. It wasn't long before Jacob was fast asleep.

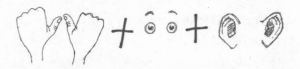

CHAPTER 8

First thing in the morning, Jacob and Cindy ran down to the engine room to see Morgenbesser. He had just cooked himself two eggs by putting a pan on top of the engine. They told him about finding the parrot and how Mr. Scrounger appeared and took it into his room.

"How very strange," said Morgenbesser, rubbing his head with his enormous hand. "Why would Mr. Scrounger have a bird when he doesn't like pets? It's very peculiar. I'm glad you've told me. Keep your eyes open for anything else unusual."

Jacob and Cindy told him they would and hurried

back up the stairs. As they went to join their parents for breakfast, Jacob thought about how nice it would be to have a parrot as a pet. But then, he thought it would be nice to have almost any animal as a pet. He'd never had one.

After breakfast, Mr. Scrounger called the children to the deck once more. "Today I've got some real fun lined up for you kids," he said. "First we're going to play pinball."

"I love pinball!" said Daniel.

"Then we're going to watch three Godzilla movies."

"Those are the best," said Marfa.

"Do we get to play pinball too?" said Jacob. "Do we?"

"And watch movies?" said Cindy.

"Oh no, pinball is much too hard for children your size. And Godzilla movies are too scary. I have a special treat for the two of you. As for you older children, off you go to the games room. And you two can come with me."

Jacob Two-Two looked at Cindy, who just shrugged. After all, their parents didn't believe them. There was nothing they could do but go with Mr. Scrounger. He took them along the deck to a metal door. "Are you ready?" he said excitedly. "One, two, three – *ta-da!*"

Mr. Scrounger opened the metal door. It was a closet. In the closet were buckets and mops.

"What are these for?" Cindy asked.

"The two of you get to continue to act like real sailors. You're going to swab the deck!"

"What does that mean? What does that mean?" asked Jacob, who had never heard of such a thing.

"You fill the pails with soapy water and use the mops to clean the floor. The decks need to shine like glass. Now here's a bucket and a mop for each of you. We'll just fill the buckets with soap and water at the sink here. Now you're all set to have yourselves a swell time."

Jacob thought that swabbing the deck did look like fun, at least sort of. And it was fun for a while, as he and Cindy plopped their mops into the buckets and swished them along the deck. But then Jacob's arms began to get sore. Not long after that, his back began to hurt. A little while later, he got cramps in his hands. But he and Cindy kept at it, moving along the deck.

Some of the adults were sitting in deck chairs reading books or magazines. Without looking, they lifted their feet so that Jacob could swab underneath them. All except one, who said, "Ahoy, matey, you almost scrubbed my shoes." It was Jacob's father.

"Dad, Dad!" Jacob cried. "Mr. Scrounger is making us swab the deck!"

"Just like real sailors, eh? You're pretty lucky kids. You enjoy yourselves now." Jacob's father closed his eyes.

Jacob considered how to convince his father that swabbing the deck wasn't much fun after an hour or two, but then his father began to snore. So he stuck his mop back in the pail and kept swabbing.

Finally, he and Cindy reached the end of the deck. Looking back, they could see the deck sparkling in the sunlight. "I see you've finished here," said Mr. Scrounger, who seemed to pop up from nowhere. "You've done an excellent job. Now all you have to do is swab the lower deck."

"The lower deck! My arms are tired," moaned Cindy.

"No complaining now. Real sailors don't whine. Pick up your buckets and mops and follow me." Mr. Scrounger took them down to the lower deck and left them to swab once more.

"I'm so tired," Cindy said. "I don't know how we

can do this deck too." Just then a door opened slowly. Jacob and Cindy stopped to see who it was.

"Morgenbesser!" Jacob cried. The enormous man smiled. He was so tall, he had to lean over so his head wouldn't bang the top of the doorway.

"I heard about you two swabbing the decks. That's not easy work for people your size. So I thought I'd give you a hand." And before Jacob and Cindy could even say "Thank you," Morgenbesser went to work. He picked up one mop in each hand, dunked them into the buckets, and began to swab at twice the speed as they did. In a jiffy, he was done.

"That was amazing," Cindy said.

"Now I better get back to the engine room before Mr. Scrounger sees me. I don't want to lose my job. See you later!" He put down the mops and squeezed back through the door. Jacob and Cindy looked at each other and grinned.

"Hurray for Morgenbesser! Hurray for Morgenbesser!" Jacob chanted. Then the door opened, and out came Mr. Scrounger with a scowl on his face.

"What, standing about when you're supposed to be working? This won't do at all."

"But we've finished, we've finished," Jacob said.

"Impossible. Let me see . . . but you have! Well, you two are even better sailors than I thought. In that case, I better give you another job."

"Another?" Cindy moaned.

"That's right. How about the two of you clean my cabin. It's an awful mess and Captain Sparkletooth is doing an inspection today. He loves doing inspections – it's what he does best. I'm sure the two of you can get my cabin in shipshape. Come along then, there's no time to waste!"

Just about the last thing that Jacob wanted to do was clean Mr. Scrounger's room, but he and Cindy followed behind. Mr. Scrounger opened his door and said "Get to it now, and no lollygagging."

"He certainly is right about it being a mess," said Cindy, when they were alone. "Even my room never gets this bad." There were dirty coffee cups everywhere, the garbage can was overflowing with candy wrappers, and newspapers were strewn all over the floor. Green and yellow feathers from the parrot floated everywhere.

"Hello, Polly. Hello," said Jacob.

"*Apple sauce in your underpants! Apple sauce in your underpants,*" said the parrot, perched on a wooden stand.

The two of them got to work. Cindy threw things into a big garbage bag, while Jacob piled up copies of *Shipwreck Monthly*. Every so often, the parrot would talk to them. *"Clean your ears!"* it would say. *"Big feet are good for dancing!"*

"Hey, Jacob, look at this," Cindy said. She came over and showed Jacob what she was holding. It was a black eye patch. "Why would Mr. Scrounger have that?" she wondered aloud. "There's nothing wrong with his eye."

"Maybe it's for a costume party," said Jacob.

"Does Mr. Scrounger look like the sort of person who goes to costume parties?"

"No, he doesn't. No, he doesn't."

"I think we better talk to Morgenbesser."

Jacob agreed that it was a good idea. The two friends rushed to finish their cleaning. Then they left Mr. Scrounger's cabin and hurried down to the engine room. The metal door was so heavy, it took the two of them to pull it open. There was Morgenbesser shoveling coal into the furnace, his muscles straining. He looked just as enormous as the first time Jacob had seen him, but Jacob wasn't afraid of him anymore.

When Morgenbesser saw them, he smiled and put down his shovel. "Hello, Jacob. Hello, Cindy. I was just going to take a break for tea. Would you like to join me?"

Cindy curtsied. "Why, I'd love to," she said.

"Me too, me too," Jacob added.

Morgenbesser already had the kettle on the furnace, and it started to whistle. He made the tea and took a baking pan from atop the furnace. Jacob could smell the freshly baked cookies. Morgenbesser set the teacups and a plate of cookies on his checkers table, and the three of them sat on the barrels.

"Oh good, the cookies didn't burn this time," Morgenbesser said. "Do have some. I hope Mr. Scrounger hasn't put you to work again."

"He has, he has," Jacob said. "We found something while cleaning his room."

"What did you find?" Morgenbesser asked, placing a whole cookie in his mouth.

"A black eye patch," Cindy said.

Morgenbesser chewed thoughtfully. "First a parrot and now an eye patch. So who wears an eye patch and goes around with a parrot?"

"I know! I know!" Jacob said. "A pirate does! A pirate does!"

"Exactly. But what would the first mate be doing with these things? The last person you want to meet while sailing on the high seas is a pirate. You two have done good work. We better be extra careful."

"These are lovely cookies," said Cindy. Jacob could see that she really did have awfully good manners.

CHAPTER 9

Jacob Two-Two and Cindy went up to the deck. Jacob said, "Will you show me your treasure now, will you?"

"Yes, I will," Cindy said. "But you must remember not to tell anyone."

"I won't, I won't."

"It's right here in my pocket."

But before Cindy could show Jacob, someone began calling to them. "Jacob Two-Two! Cindy! *Yoo-hoo!*" It was Captain Sparkletooth. He was waving to them from beside the wheelhouse. "This is a perfect time for both of you to have your photograph taken with me. I'm sure you'll agree that I look particularly handsome today."

Near him was Mr. Scrounger with a camera on a tripod. Jacob had no desire to be photographed with Captain Sparkletooth. But he didn't want to hurt the captain's feelings, so he and Cindy went over. A heavy mist hung over the ocean. It was so thick that Jacob could hardly see five feet beyond the rail of the ship.

"You first, Jacob Two-Two," said the captain. "Don't be shy now. Move a little closer. Now when you get this photograph, Jacob, don't be surprised if you look pale and insignificant next to my magnificent self. Everyone does. Have you got all of me in focus, Mr. Scrounger? Not just my nose like last time."

"Almost," said Mr. Scrounger.

"What's that out there?" Cindy pointed past the rail of the ship. "There's something there in the mist."

"Don't move or you'll spoil the shot," said Mr. Scrounger. But Jacob turned his head to look. Cindy was right, there was something out there. A dark form slowly emerged from the mist.

"Why, this is most annoying," Captain Sparkletooth said. "This was going to be one of the best photographs of me ever. I don't see what can be so interesting out there."

Jacob could just make out the carved figurehead of a mermaid. "It's a ship! It's a ship!" he cried. As it became more visible, Jacob could see that it was a very old ship, the kind with three tall masts and big sails. He could also see cannons – dozens of them – lined up along the ship's side.

"If anyone is going to greet the captain of another ship, that person ought to be me," Captain Sparkletooth said. "In fact, I have a speech prepared for just such an occasion. Mr. Scrounger, where is my bullhorn? Ah, here it is on this hook." The captain put the bullhorn to his mouth. "This is the captain of the SS *Spring-a-Leak* calling. I welcome you to . . . to . . . wherever we are. In recognition of the brotherhood of all sailors, we offer our hospitality to you all. I believe we have muffins and hot chocolate."

Now Jacob could see the flag waving from the top of one of the masts. It was a black flag, with a skull and crossbones on it – the Jolly Roger! "It's a pirate ship. It's a pirate ship!" Jacob said.

"Nonsense, Jacob," said Captain Sparkletooth. "There haven't been pirates in these waters for two hundred years. Do you think I'd be out here if there were? There must be some other reason. I know!

They're making a movie. I hear that pirate movies are very popular these days. Perhaps the stars would like to have their picture taken with me. . . ."

The captain's words were drowned out by an explosion. *Bazoom!* Something whizzed over their heads and splashed into the water on the other side of the SS *Spring-a-Leak*.

"It's a cannonball!" Jacob cried. "They're firing at us! They're firing!"

"Firing?" said Captain Sparkletooth. "I'm shocked. How rude. There is only one thing for a brave and handsome captain such as myself to do. Surrender! Somebody wave a white flag. We don't have one? How inconvenient. Here, I'll wave my jacket."

But by the time the captain had undone all the brass buttons, the pirate ship was already alongside the SS *Spring-a-Leak*. A gangplank was laid across the rails, and two very dirty pirates in bare feet stepped nimbly across, holding out their swords. "Prepare to meet the greatest pirate of them all!" one of them announced. "Introducing our leader, Crossbones!"

Crossbones? Jacob shivered at the very sound of the name. Out of the mist emerged a man in a pirate hat and leather boots. As the pirate crossed over the

gangway, Jacob saw his eye patch, his grizzled beard, and the cutlass tucked in his broad belt. He swaggered as he walked, his big stomach swaying with each step. With a grunt he began to pull himself over the rail of the SS *Spring-a-Leak*. There was a loud ripping sound.

"Tarnation!" growled Crossbones. "I believe I have rendered a tear in my lower garment."

"What did he just say?" asked Captain Sparkle-tooth.

"He ripped his pants," said one of the other pirates.

Crossbones stepped up to the Captain and leaned on his sword. Captain Sparkletooth, his teeth chattering with fear, removed his cap. "Oh, dear, Mr. Crossbones, you have quite a reputation. A terrible reputation."

"You flatter me. I believe I am even blushing," said Crossbones. "You have done well to surrender, Captain Sparkletooth. Otherwise, I would have had to mar, soil, besmear – in other words, stain – that scrumptious uniform of yours. With blood, I mean."

"I don't like the sight of blood, especially my own," said Captain Sparkletooth. "But if I might ask a question, why are you here?"

"*Aargh*! That's the question, ain't it, boys?"

"Aye," agreed the other pirates, grinning so that their black teeth showed. "A good question, ha-ha!"

"Aye, I'll answer it, too. But first, pirates, bar those doors to the lower decks. I hear people coming up the stairs." The pirates did as they were told. Jacob could hear the voices of other passengers, including his own parents. "I'll tell you why we're here," Crossbones went on. "We've come for the swag, the snatch, the booty – in other words, the treasure."

"Yes, the treasure, the treasure!" sang the pirates.

"I don't know of any treasure aboard the SS *Spring-a-Leak*. Why do you think there's treasure here?"

"Because I have a spy on your ship."

"A spy aboard the SS *Spring-a-Leak*? Outrageous. When I find out who the spy is, I'm going to take away his dessert for a week. Make that two weeks. Mr. Scrounger, do you know who the spy is?"

"I do, Captain."

"Don't tell me, let me guess. Is it the bosun?"

"No, Captain."

"Is it the cook?"

"No, Captain."

"I know who it is! I know who it is!" Jacob said.

"You couldn't possibly know," said Captain Sparkletooth. "You're going to say something ridiculous, like it's Mr. Scrounger."

"But it *is* Mr. Scrounger! It *is* Mr. Scrounger!"

The captain sighed. "Mr. Scrounger, tell Jacob that it isn't you."

"But it *is* me," Mr. Scrounger said.

"Stop fooling around. This is serious," said the captain.

"No, I mean it," said Mr. Scrounger. "Hold on, I'll prove it."

Mr. Scrounger hurried away while everyone else stood waiting. Even Crossbones, who was muttering under his breath while he cleaned his nails with the tip of his sword. Mr. Scrounger appeared again, this time with the parrot on his shoulder and the black eye patch around his head.

"See! See! I'm a pirate, too. Don't I look like one now? Say something, parrot," he cried.

The parrot tilted its head, clacked its beak, and squawked, *"Pirates and pickles cost only a nickel! Pirates and pickles cost only a nickel!"*

"First of all," said Crossbones, stepping up to Mr. Scrounger, "there can't be two of us wearing an eye patch. That would be preposterous, asinine, and a mockery – in other words, dumb. You take yours off."

"Oh, rats," said Mr. Scrounger. As he took the eye patch off, he thwacked himself on the ear.

"But why, Mr. Scrounger?" asked Captain Sparkletooth. "Why would you betray us? Especially when I am so much more handsome than he is!"

"I'll tell you why," answered Mr. Scrounger. "Because I'm tired of watching you comb your hair while you admire yourself in the mirror. I'm tired of taking *your* photograph. I want to be noticed for a change."

"*I notice your feet smell! I notice your feet smell!*" squawked the parrot.

"Please get that bird to shut up," said Crossbones. "We've got pirate work to do here."

"No, you don't," said a commanding voice. Jacob recognized it immediately. He looked up, and in the ship's rigging he saw none other than the intrepid Shapiro and the fearless O'Toole, their shirts emblazoned with the words *Child Power*, their capes fluttering behind them.

"We thought our work was done," said the fearless

O'Toole, "but it seems that we've got more cleaning up to do."

Crossbones looked at them and shrugged. "Tie them up," he said.

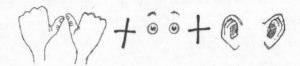

CHAPTER 10

Jacob Two-Two watched in horror as the pirates pulled the intrepid Shapiro and the fearless O'Toole down from the rigging and tied their hands behind their backs.

"Mr. Scrounger," called Crossbones, "take the wheel. Steer a course thirty degrees west. Make sure our own ship follows us."

"Aye, aye, Crossbones," said Mr. Scrounger, going to the wheelhouse.

"Where are we going? Where are we going?" asked Jacob.

Crossbones gave Jacob a nasty smile. "It is always

best to remove a nuisance," he said. "I happen to know a most exquisite stretch of beach not far from here that I'm sure these two will enjoy. A shame it happens to be on a desert island."

"A desert island? Without food and water? They'll starve. They'll starve."

"Do you think I care? If I weren't cruel and ruthless, I wouldn't be called Crossbones, would I? I'd be called Henry or George. I just don't know what they teach you in school these days."

"I had an uncle named Henry," said one of the pirates. "And an aunt named George."

"Be quiet, you. I can see the island now. One drooping palm tree to keep them company. Send the two troublemakers down."

Jacob watched in dismay as the intrepid Shapiro and the fearless O'Toole were put into a lifeboat with one of the pirates and lowered to the water. The pirate rowed to a tiny island with a single palm tree and a single rock on it. He untied the intrepid Shapiro and the fearless O'Toole, drew his sword, and forced them out of the boat. Once the Infamous Two were out of the boat, the pirate rowed back to the ship.

"Good luck to ya," called Crossbones, laughing heartily. "All right, Mr. Scrounger, take us away."

The ship began to move. As he looked down at the helpless duo, Jacob noticed one of the lower cabin windows opening. A canvas bag flew out the window and landed on the island. It opened up and out spilled bottles of water, boxes of crackers, chocolate bars, and other supplies. Through the window, a big, muscled arm appeared and gave the thumbs-up sign. It was Morgenbesser!

"Good old Morgenbesser," Jacob whispered.

"Eh, what's that? What are you mumbling?" asked Crossbones.

"Just that the morning couldn't be better, couldn't be better," Jacob said.

"You are a mixed-up kid. It isn't even morning. And things are going to get much worse. Captain Sparkletooth, hand over the treasure."

"But I told you, we have no treasure," the captain said. "We have a load of freeze-dried cottage cheese. We have seven barrels of prunes. But we don't have any treasure on this ship."

"Of course you do. Mr. Scrounger informed,

enlightened, and apprised me – that is, he told me so. Scrounger, get out here!"

Mr. Scrounger came out of the wheelhouse. The parrot squawked, *"I love to dance the tango! I love to dance the tango!"*

"You'll be roasting in the oven if you don't shut your beak," said Crossbones. "Now, tell us about the treasure, Mr. Scrounger."

"Walking about the ship, I heard somebody whispering. I don't know who it was, but I know for certain that somebody is hiding treasure on this ship."

Crossbones put his hand on the hilt of his sword. "We better get everyone here then. Pirates, unbar that door and let the other passengers up on deck."

The pirates opened the door and the passengers filed out. "Jacob, are you alright?" cried his mother. His father rushed toward him too, followed by Daniel and Marfa.

Mrs. Snootcastle hurried up to Cindy. "All I can say is this shows some very bad manners," said Mrs. Snootcastle.

"Everyone here?" said Crossbones. "Good. And now if the person who has the treasure will take one step forward, we can have all of this settled by dinnertime."

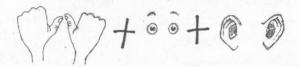

CHAPTER 11

Jacob knew what they were thinking: *Who has the treasure?* Of course he knew. The treasure was in Cindy's pocket. All she had to do was give it to Crossbones, and he and his dastardly pirates would put away their daggers and swords and sail away on their pirate ship.

Jacob looked over at Cindy. She stood by her mother, staring down at her shoes. She wasn't going to tell the pirates about her treasure! Should he, Jacob Two-Two, do something? Should he tell the pirates? Jacob knew that the treasure must be precious to Cindy if she didn't want to say anything.

How would he like it if somebody made him give up something he cared about? Jacob decided not to say anything.

At last, the eldest of the Bubov Brothers spoke. "We have the treasure."

"Yes, we do," said the middle brother.

"Definitely," said the youngest.

"What is it?" asked Crossbones. "Is it gold? Is it silver? Rubies? Diamonds?"

"It's our special no-slip acrobat shoes," replied the eldest brother. "We couldn't perform without them. We'll give them to you."

"I don't want your old shoes," said Crossbones. "And that isn't treasure. Someone else must have it."

"Alright, go ahead and tell them what the treasure is," said Hector the ventriloquist dummy, rolling his eyes at Percy Swishbottom.

"No, I won't," said Percy.

"Don't be a bigger dummy than me. Give it to them."

"Fine." Percy sighed. He reached into his jacket and pulled out a small pamphlet. Jacob read the title: *How to Throw Your Voice and Amaze Your Friends.* "I mailed in a coupon from a comic book to get this.

It taught me how to be a ventriloquist. It's the most valuable thing I have."

"I don't want to throw my voice, but I might throw your dummy overboard!" growled Crossbones.

"No problem," said the dummy. "I float."

"It is my turn to confess," said Mr. Peabody. "I have the treasure. Here it is – my greatest invention ever!"

Mr. Peabody unfolded a large blueprint with a complex drawing of a large box covered in buttons, levers, and switches. Attached to the box by mechanical arms were a baseball bat, an umbrella, and a bicycle pump. Inside the box was an even more complicated series of wheels and belts and computer chips.

"What does it do?" asked one of the pirates.

"I don't know yet," Mr. Peabody admitted.

"Put your paper away," snarled Crossbones. "It's worthless."

Jacob's father took a step forward. "I don't have a treasure on me, but I could make you one," he said.

Crossbones squinted an eye at Jacob's father. "What sort of treasure?"

"A book. I can write a book and make you the villain. People all over the world will read it and tremble at the very description of you."

"Villain, you say? I like the sound of that."

"Oh, put me in the book too!" cried Captain Sparkletooth. "I'm sure it would be greatly improved by your mentioning how handsome I am."

"I admit, it's tempting," said Crossbones. "But it's not good enough. What we want is treasure. *Real* treasure. Otherwise we wouldn't be pirates. We'd be like regular people, who take baths and drink capuccinos."

Mrs. Snootcastle sniffed. "I don't know who has the treasure, but I know that person is certainly not someone with good breeding and manners. When I find out who it is, you can be sure that I will have nothing to do with that person again."

Tears welled up in Cindy's eyes. Jacob felt sorry for his friend. And he thought that his father and the others had shown real courage. He wanted to help too, but he couldn't think of anything.

"I know what to do," Crossbones sneered. "We're going to have to resort to more drastic measures. Captain Sparkletooth, you are going to have to walk the plank!"

"*Oooohh,*" said the pirates.

Captain Sparkletooth's eyes grew wide. His upper lip began to tremble. "Please no," he pleaded. "Don't make me walk the plank. Can't you choose someone else, someone less handsome? I'm sure it would be much more effective if you chose someone people actually cared about. Then you'd find out who has the treasure!"

"I've read a book about pirates," said Noah. "They never really did make people walk the plank. It's a myth."

"I don't care if it's a myth," said Crossbones. "People expect it of us. But Captain Sparkletooth has a good point. Someone else would suit me better." He paced back and forth. "I'll just pick someone. Should I pick you? Or you? I know – I'll pick *you!*"

Crossbones swiveled on his boot heels and pointed a bony finger right at Jacob. "What is your name, boy?" he demanded.

"It's Jacob Two-Two. It's Jacob Two-Two."

"You're as bad as that revolting parrot, the way you repeat yourself. You will walk the plank."

His father stepped forward and put his arms around Jacob. "Leave my boy out of it. He's only two plus two plus two years old. Choose me instead."

"Or me," said Jacob's mother.

But the two pirates came forward and pulled Jacob away. "Sorry," Crossbones said, "but I find the boy a far superior, preferable, and most excellent choice. In other words, he's going. Now hurry up, we haven't got all day."

Jacob tried not to look afraid. "If you don't hurt anyone else, I'll walk the plank, I'll walk." One of the pirates helped him up onto the plank stretched over the water. Jacob took a step forward. He remembered that it would soon be his birthday. He would be two plus two plus two *plus one*. Well, he didn't have to worry about his birthday now, since he wasn't going to reach it.

"What are you waiting for?" asked Crossbones.

"Hurry up, or I'll send your pesky family with you."

He took another step and then another. The wooden plank started to bend downwards. Two more steps and he was halfway to the end of the plank. Below him swirled the dark sea. He closed his eyes and shuffled forward until he was standing at the edge.

"Stop!" cried a voice. "Stop! I have the treasure! Don't make Jacob Two-Two walk any farther!"

Jacob knew it was Cindy calling. Crossbones started to laugh. "I knew you were all softies! Alright, boy, come back now. Count yourself lucky."

Jacob felt a huge relief as he walked carefully backwards until he was on the ship again.

"Cynthia Francis Louise Snootcastle!" cried her mother. "Don't tell me that you've brought the family jewels with you. They are supposed to be in the safe at home. Why, they were there just the day before we left. I was running my fingers through them – I mean, I was checking them for safekeeping."

"No, Mother," said Cindy. "I have a different treasure in my pocket. I didn't want you to know about it."

"Didn't want me to know? Well, well. My own daughter has a treasure that she doesn't wish to share

with me. I'm speechless. I'm dumbfounded. I'm at a loss for words."

"And yet, Madam," said Jacob's father, "you still speak."

"Enough of this chitchat," said Crossbones. "Come on, child, show me your treasure. Show it, I say!"

"Alright," Cindy said, stepping forward. She put her hand carefully into her pocket, moved it around, and then drew it out. She turned her hand over, opening her fingers. And there on her palm was . . . *a mouse!*

Such an adorable mouse, Jacob thought. The mouse sniffed the air, perked up its fuzzy ears, and cleaned

its whiskers. Cindy stroked its soft head, whispering "That's a good Treasure."

"What is it? My eyes aren't what they used to be," said Crossbones. He and Mr. Scrounger bent over at the same time, knocking heads. "Ouch! Get back, you scurvy dog! You hurt my noggin!"

"And mine," said Mr. Scrounger, rubbing his own head.

Crossbones bent over again, this time lifting up his eye patch. "Now let me take a look at what you've got. Is it silver? Pearls? A little closer . . . ah, I see now. . . . It's a . . . a . . . *mouse?*" Crossbones sprang back, crashing into his fellow pirates. "Get that thing away from me!" he cried.

"Are you afraid of mice? Are you afraid of mice?" Jacob asked.

"I'm not afraid of anything. I was just surprised, that's all. But I don't understand. Why did you say you have treasure?" asked Crossbones.

"Because her *name* is Treasure," Cindy said.

"You mean there's no real treasure on the ship? No gold, no diamonds, or rubies? *Aargh!* Mr. Scrounger, you have failed me!"

"I'm sorry, Crossbones," Mr. Scrounger said meekly.

"Please don't put me in irons. At least I've found two pirates to join your crew, just like you asked."

"Right, I did ask you to do that. Which ones have you been training?"

"Those two." Mr. Scrounger pointed at Jacob and Cindy. "I chose the youngest, just like you said."

"Excellent. You two are just the right age to teach how to be a pirate. Why, I was just a tot, a moppet, a lad – in short, a kid – myself when I started. Bring them aboard our ship, Mr. Scrounger. We'll leave the rest behind and good riddance to them."

"Now wait a minute. You can't take my son," said Jacob's father.

"Nor my daughter, even if she has been naughty," said Mrs. Snootcastle.

"Just watch me," Crossbones said. "Pirates, throw those parents below. If I say these two are going to be pirates, then pirates they'll be!"

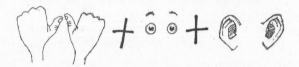

CHAPTER 12

As soon as they were aboard their pirate ship, Crossbones ordered the crew to pull up anchor and raise the sails. Jacob and Cindy watched as the pirates scrambled up the masts and untied the ropes, the sails unfurling in the wind. Within moments, the old wooden ship was racing across the water. As they worked, the pirates sang.

We don't like washing behind our ears,
or learning our multiplication.
When our noses drip, we blow in our sleeves
and we spit for relaxation!

It's the pirate life for us, hey ho!
The pirate life for us!

Our shirts are ruffly, our scarves are rags,
our trousers are torn at the bottom.
We like to wear earings and even tattoos,
but now everybody's got 'em!

It's the pirate life for us, hey ho!
The pirate life for us!

We search for treasure on the high seas,
gold and silver and more.
But we ain't found nothing for all our work,
and this life is becoming a bore!

Enough of the pirate life, hey ho!
Enough of the pirate life!

"What's that you're singing?" asked Crossbones menacingly. The pirates began to tremble and switched to a different song. "That's better. Mr. Scrounger, give me a report."

"We're going full sail, sir," Mr. Scrounger said. "We couldn't go faster if we put our feet in to paddle."

"You're a bad boy and you won't get any supper!" squawked the parrot.

"Shut that thing up."

"Yes, sir. Just one question, Crossbones."

"What is it?"

"Why are we in such a hurry? I mean, we're racing at top speed across the Atlantic Ocean. Do we have a reason?"

Crossbones rubbed his chin. He looked to the left and to the right. "Hmm, good point," he mumbled. He cupped his hands to his mouth and shouted "STOP THE SHIP!" so loud, Jacob and Cindy jumped.

Once more, the pirates sprang into action. They pulled down the sails and threw out the anchor. "Gather around, mates," Crossbones called. The crew formed a circle around him.

"Are we going to sing more songs?" asked a pirate.

"No, you nincompoop. We've got a serious problem. As pirates, our job is to find treasure. But we haven't any idea where to look."

The pirates scratched their heads. They scratched under their arms. None of them could think of where any treasure might be. Crossbones declared that the ship would stay right where it was until somebody thought of a place to look.

"In the meantime, maybe we could have a wee nip of rum," a pirate said hesitantly. "After all, next to treasure, pirates love rum."

"Rum, rum! A wee nip of rum!" chanted the pirates. Crossbones, who liked his rum as much as the next pirate, agreed. A barrel was brought from below. As they had no glasses, each pirate put his mouth under the spout of the barrel for three seconds. He got to the back of the line to wait for another turn. Very soon, the pirates were happily singing again.

It's the pirate life for us, hey ho!
The pirate life for us!

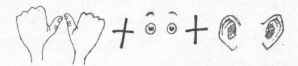

CHAPTER 13

While the pirates were singing and drinking rum, Crossbones gave Jacob and Cindy jobs to do. As the youngest pirates on the ship, they were given the worst chores. First, they had to clean seagull poop off the wooden figurehead attached to the bow of the ship. Leaning over the edge, they reached down with soapy mops to scrub the mermaid. When they were finally done, they returned to discover that all the pirates were asleep, including Crossbones.

"What if we never get away?" said Jacob. "We could become teenaged pirates and then adult pirates and then old pirates. We could!"

"I know. If only we could think of something," said Cindy.

Jacob heard a sound. He listened harder. Someone was calling his name. It had to be his imagination – after all, they were floating in the middle of the ocean. But then he heard it again.

"Do you hear that? Do you hear that?" Jacob asked.

"I do," said Cindy. "I think it's coming from the water."

The two friends hurried to the side of the ship. When they looked down, they saw a raft made of wooden logs tied together with vines. On the bobbing raft were none other than the intrepid Shapiro and the fearless O'Toole! Their capes fluttered in the breeze.

"Here, take this," called Shapiro.

Shapiro held out a piece of paper. But when Jacob stretched his hand over the side of the ship, he couldn't reach it. He leaned farther and farther over the side – and then he slipped!

"I've got you!" said Cindy, holding on to Jacob. Jacob reached down and grabbed the paper. Cindy pulled him back up again.

"What do I do with it? What do I do with it?" Jacob asked.

"Hide it!" said Shapiro.

"But not too well!" added O'Toole. Their raft began to drift away from the ship. The Infamous Two waved until they could be seen no more. Jacob and Cindy examined the piece of paper. It was torn at the edges, stained with tea, and smudged with dirt. On it was a drawing of a large island. On the island was an X marked in crayon. It looked just like the sort of map that Jacob's older brothers and sisters made when they were pretending to be explorers.

Jacob did what he was told. He rolled up the map and put it in his pocket, but he let the end stick out. A large wave splashed over the rear of the ship, drenching the pirates with cold water and waking them up. Crossbones cursed and kicked Mr. Scrounger, who cursed and kicked the pirate next to him, who did the same – all the way down the line.

Stretching, Crossbones noticed Jacob and Cindy. "Finished your job, have you? I'm sure I can find something else that nobody wants to do. Wait a minute, what's that in your pocket?"

"Nothing, nothing," Jacob said, pretending to hide the paper.

"You can't fool me." Crossbones snatched the paper away and unfolded it. "Hmm," he said, peering closely. "Torn edges. Tea stains. Crayon mark. Why, this looks like a treasure map! Where did you get it?"

"It was floating on the water," Cindy said quickly.

"This is it, mates! We're saved! We've got real pirate work to do at last. We're going after this treasure!"

The pirates linked arms and began to dance in a circle, kicking up their heels.

It's the pirate life for us, hey ho!
The pirate life for us!"

"Stop that racket! Now, according to the map we've got to head due south until we come to a large island. Mr. Scrounger, take the wheel!"

The pirates snapped into action. Crossbones gave Jacob and Cindy the job of polishing the cannons. He also gave each of them a hard biscuit and a slice of lemon. "That's so you don't get scurvy," he told them. Cindy shared her biscuit with Treasure. *A mouse is a pretty small pet,* Jacob thought, *but it's certainly better than no pet at all.*

"Brush your teeth with soya sauce! Brush your teeth with soya sauce!" squawked the parrot.

They had not been working long before a pirate up in the crow's nest called out "Land ahoy!" Jacob and Cindy hurried to the bow of the ship, where they could see the island in the distance. It was a lot bigger than the island where Crossbones had left the intrepid Shapiro and the fearless O'Toole. Mr. Scrounger called on the pirate crew to drop anchor near the shoreline. Then he called on them to prepare a rowboat.

"Come on, you two squirts," Crossbones said. "You found the map. Maybe you'll be of some use finding the treasure."

Jacob and Cindy got into the rowboat with Crossbones, Mr. Scrounger, and two other pirates, and the boat was lowered into the water. Another boatload of pirates followed behind. As the pirates rowed toward the shore, they began to sing.

> *We're pirates in a boat, hurrah!*
> *We hope to keep afloat, hurrah!*
> *But if we start to sink, hurrah!*
> *We'll think this job does stink, hurrah!*

"Stop that singing!" Crossbones demanded. "I don't understand why pirates have to sing so much. Now pull up onto the beach."

The sailors jumped into the shallows and pulled the boats up onto the shore. Jacob and Cindy stepped onto the sand after Crossbones and Mr. Scrounger. Crossbones held out the map and examined it.

"I believe you're holding it upside down," said Mr. Scrounger.

"I knew that." Crossbones quickly turned it over. "I was testing you. Right, then. We go forward for thirty paces, cross a stream, zigzag through a swamp, around a palm tree, walk up a hill, and it's on the other side. That sounds simple enough. Follow me!"

Crossbones pulled out his sword, held it aloft, and began to walk. The rest straggled after, with Jacob and Cindy coming up behind. "What do you think will happen when we get there?" Cindy asked.

"Maybe the pirates will fall into a hole," said Jacob. "Or get caught in a net, a big net."

"We better not get caught too," Cindy said. Crossbones counted out thirty paces, then crossed the stream, then zigzagged through the swamp. Mosquitoes swarmed around them, making the pirates dance as they slapped at themselves. Then they went around a palm tree and started to climb the hill.

The hill was big and high, and soon the pirates, who were in bad shape, began panting for breath. "We're almost there, lads," puffed Crossbones, shakily raising his sword. "When we get to the top of this hill, we'll be able to see where the treasure is. Onward!"

Forward they went. All of them reached the top of the hill at the same time. And all of them stopped, including Jacob. Because what they saw wasn't treasure at all.

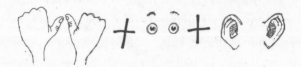

CHAPTER 14

At the bottom of the hill, Jacob saw a stage. A big stage. A curtain stitched together from old sailor's uniforms stretched between two tall palm trees. Above the curtain, made out of twisted sticks, were the words *Treasure Theater*.

"What is this, some kind of deception, ruse, gimmick – in short, a trick?" asked Crossbones. "Draw your swords, mates. We'll approach with caution, and if it's an ambush, we'll cut 'em down!"

Some of the pirates had trouble getting their swords out of their belts, but at last they were all ready. Jacob didn't think they looked very brave. In fact, they looked scared out of their wits. Their knees knocked together and their teeth chattered. And when they heard a loud sound, like an out-of-tune trumpet, they jumped into the air.

"*Bbbbttthhheeeww!*" the noise went again. At that moment, two people slipped out from behind the curtain. It was none other than the intrepid Shapiro and the fearless O'Toole, wearing their towel capes and their glowing *Child Power* shirts. Shapiro was holding a big conch shell. He raised it to his lips and blew into it.

"Ladies and gentlemen!" cried O'Toole. "Pirates, traitors, and captives! Our show is about to begin. If all of you would take your seats, you will see some of the most spectacular, most daring performances ever attempted on an uninhabited island. What you see today will leave you with memories to treasure your whole life!"

"Memories?" muttered Crossbones under his breath. "What sort of treasure is that?"

"Our first act," called out Shapiro, "comes direct from the Ural Mountains. Please put your hands together and give a big welcome to . . . *the Bubov Brothers!*"

The pirates sat and began to clap. "Not so fast," Crossbones said. "This could still be a trick." But he too sat down. Jacob and Cindy looked at each other, then sat too. Slowly the curtain jerked open to reveal a trapeze hanging in the air by vines. The Bubov Brothers tumbled onto the stage, shouting to one another. They rose quickly and spread out their arms. Then the middle brother got onto the shoulders of the eldest brother, and the youngest brother got onto the shoulders of the middle brother. The youngest brother juggled three coconuts and then added a boot, a soup ladle, a sailor's cap, and a framed photograph of Captain Sparkletooth. The pirates whooped with delight.

Next the youngest brother grabbed hold of the trapeze and began to swing. He executed a series of gymnastic moves, then hooked his feet over the bar, swung down, and grabbed his middle brother's hands. He swung him up into the air and let go. The middle brother did three somersaults in the air, landing in his older brother's arms.

The pirates cheered as the curtain closed. Even Crossbones was clapping.

After the Bubov Brothers came Percy Swishbottom and his dummy, Hector, who was wearing a pirate hat

and a patch over his eye. The pirates in the audience pointed and laughed.

"Why are you dressed like that?" Percy asked Hector.

"Isn't it obvious?" replied Hector. "Because I want to be a pirate."

"Why do you want to be a pirate?"

"Well, I figured I might as well. I've already got a wooden leg." The real pirates howled.

"What kind of wood are you made out of anyway?" Percy asked.

"Guess."

"You want me to guess?"

"No, I just said the word 'guess' for no reason. Of course I want you to guess."

"Maple?"

"*Mais, non,*" said the dummy.

"Oak?"

"What a joke!"

"Birch?"

"A bird's perch!"

"Mahogany?"

"That's funny!"

"Alright, I give up."

"Sick of more?" asked the dummy.

"Yes, I am, so tell me what wood you're made of."

"But I just told you. I'm made out of sycamore!"

"That figures."

"Hey, it could be worse. I've got a cousin made out of nutty pine."

"Isn't that *knotty* pine?"

"You don't know my cousin."

Jacob thought that Percy Swishbottom with his dummy was the silliest act he had ever seen, but the pirates loved it. After they left the stage, Jacob was astonished to see his mother and father step through the curtains.

His father began to speak. "I shall now recite, from memory, the great poem by Sammy Cooleridge called 'The Gassy Sailor.' While I do so, my lovely wife shall make appropriate sound effects."

Jacob applauded as loud as he could. Smiling, he looked over at Cindy. He was surprised to see that she looked unhappy.

"What's wrong? What's wrong?" Jacob asked.

"I wish my mother would perform too," she said. "But she thinks that performers are low-class."

Jacob felt sorry for Cindy. When his parents finished and everyone cheered, the intrepid Shapiro and the fearless O'Toole came out again. "You are a wonderful audience," they said. "And you are in for a real treat. Tonight only, we present to you the celebrated opera singer and former star of the Hackensack Opera Company, Dame Camilia Snootcastle. She will perform the final aria in Puppinello's great tragic opera, *The Soggy Sandwich*."

"Opera?" said Cindy, her eyes growing wide. "My mother doesn't sing opera."

"Maybe she does. Maybe she does," Jacob said. And sure enough, out came Mrs. Snootcastle wearing an enormous velvet gown, her hands clasped before her. She stood at center stage, looked at the audience, took in a deep breath, and began to sing. Her voice rose higher and grew louder until the palm trees holding up the curtains began to shake and coconuts fell to the ground.

"Hurray! *Bravo!*" shouted the pirates. Several had tears in their eyes.

"That was my mother," Cindy said proudly.

"Yes it was. Yes it was." Jacob nodded happily.

Once again, out came the intrepid Shapiro and the fearless O'Toole. They announced several more acts. Mr. Peabody, the toy inventor, demonstrated his new yo-yo that let off fireworks as it spun. Except for the moment when Mr. Peabody's trousers caught on fire, it was a success. After him came Marfa and Daniel, who performed some skateboarding tricks, with Daniel crashing only once.

Then there was Captain Sparkletooth. Captain Sparkletooth brought out his collection of mirrors. He had thirty-two of them.

"Impressive," muttered the pirates.

"And finally," announced O'Toole, while Shapiro blew into the conch shell, "our final act. Making a return to the ring after years in retirement, the only man who was ever a match for The Hooded Fang, please welcome one of the great wrestlers of all time, *The Mighty Morgenbesser!*"

Jacob watched as the curtains parted to reveal his friend. Dressed in green wrestling leotards, Morgenbesser flexed his arm muscles to show how strong he was. O'Toole declared that since there was no one on the island strong enough to wrestle him, Morgenbesser would take on all three Bubov Brothers at the same time.

The brothers came out and surrounded Morgenbesser, clenching their fists and making fierce faces. Suddenly, the eldest brother jumped onto Morgenbesser's back, while the other two grabbed Morgenbesser's arms. Soon, all three brothers were flying through the air. Fortunately, they were nimble enough to land on their feet.

Next, the brothers all rushed toward Morgenbesser, screaming loudly. Morgenbesser just crossed his arms and let them bounce off his chest. Dizzy, the brothers got up again. Then they fell back down. And got up again. And fell down again.

"The winner and still champion," said O'Toole, holding up the giant man's hand, "The Mighty Morgenbesser!"

Whistles and foot-stomping came from the audience. Jacob and Cindy made the loudest noise of anyone.

"And now," said Shapiro, "Captain Sparkletooth has a special announcement to make."

The captain came out, adjusting his white cape and smiling his sparkling smile. "I have decided to turn the SS *Spring-a-Leak* into a showboat."

"Great!" shouted the pirates. "Fantastic!"

Mr. Scrounger in the front row called out, "What's a showboat?"

"Very simple," said the captain. "It's a boat with a show on it. The boat docks in port, and people buy tickets to come aboard and watch. You see, I realize just how handsome I look up on stage. There's only one thing. Some of our performers are on their way to Canada. Their places need to be filled with new acts. We are hoping that you pirates might want to give up your life on the high seas to become performers."

"We do! We do!" shouted the pirates.

"Wait a minute," said Crossbones. He stood up and glared down at his men. "Nobody gives up being a pirate unless I say so. And I have a question. Just what sort of acts would we have?"

Now Jacob stood up. "You could put on a play!" he said. "A play about pirates! A play about pirates!"

Cindy stood up too. "You could fight with wooden swords. And you could sing pirate songs."

All of the pirates looked hopefully at Crossbones. Crossbones rubbed his beard. "That sounds like something we could do. In fact, we'd probably be better at pretending to be pirates than actually *being* pirates. What do you say, mates? Shall we wear the greasepaint and tread the boards? Shall we make the audience weep hot tears with our death scenes, sigh gently over our love scenes, and laugh heartily over our comic turns? Shall we be . . . *actors?*"

"Yes!" cried the pirates, raising their fists in the air. "Yes! Yes! YES!"

"Sour cream makes good shampoo!" squawked the parrot.

"Does that mean we're free? Does that mean we're free?" Jacob asked.

"Indeed it does," said Crossbones. "No hard feelings, I hope."

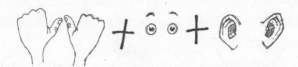

CHAPTER 15

Jacob was overjoyed to be reunited with his mother and father. Even his brothers and sisters were glad to see him. Cindy was just as happy to see her mother, and Mrs. Snootcastle was so glad to have Cindy back that she didn't even mind Treasure anymore. She told Cindy all about her career as an opera singer before she married Mr. Snootcastle and retired from the stage.

The SS *Spring-a-Leak* was waiting on the other side of the island. After they got on board, Crossbones and his pirates returned to their own ship and followed behind. Crossbones didn't want to fly the

Jolly Roger from the foremast now that they were no longer going to be real pirates. But since he didn't have any other flag, he borrowed a pair of polka-dotted boxer shorts from Captain Sparkletooth and flew them instead.

Before turning his ship into a showboat, Captain Sparkletooth had to deliver his passengers to Canada. They continued on their journey, returning to the old routine of shuffleboard games and fancy meals in the dining room. Jacob and Cindy got to play the games now too. They also visited their friend Morgenbesser down in the engine room, where they all had tea and played checkers.

One evening at dinner, Mrs. Snootcastle turned to Jacob's father and said, "I'm reading your latest book. It is not nearly as dreadful as I thought."

"Coming from you," said Jacob's father, "I consider that a great compliment."

Just before dessert, the band suddenly struck up the song "Happy Birthday." Jacob watched as Morgenbesser, dressed in a white suit, wheeled in a giant cake. Jacob's family began to sing and everyone joined in. So they hadn't forgotten his birthday after all! In fact, it was Jacob who had forgotten. For a moment he was glad, but then he remembered why he had wanted to skip it in the first place.

"Blow out the candles, Jacob," said a smiling Morgenbesser. Jacob took a big breath and began to blow. He managed to blow out all the candles himself, although Morgenbesser helped him with the last two. Everyone cheered.

Daniel said "Hey, wait a minute. Jacob isn't two plus two plus two years old anymore."

Here it comes, Jacob thought. They were going to make fun of his name. They were going to call him Jacob Two-Two Plus One after all. There was nothing he could do about it.

"You're right," said Jacob's father, ruffling his hair. "Jacob is now two plus two plus two plus *one brave boy.*"

Jacob grinned from ear to ear.

CHAPTER 16

At last the shores of Canada came into view. Jacob Two-Two stood at the rail beside Cindy as the SS *Spring-a-Leak* sailed down the Gulf of Saint Lawrence and along the Gaspé Peninsula of Quebec. Before long the port of Montreal came into view. Jacob could see a brass band playing and hundreds of people waving. As the ship docked, Jacob's father said, "I recognize that person up on the platform. That's Perry Pleaser, the prime minister of Canada."

Jacob's father was right. A red carpet was rolled along the gangway and Jacob, his family, and the other passengers walked off the ship. Jacob wondered why the prime minister was there. Perhaps it was to thank his father for writing the very important novel.

The prime minister called all of them up to the platform. "On behalf of Canada and all the civilized nations of the world," said the prime minister, "I wish to bestow these medals on Jacob Two-Two and Cindy Snootcastle. These two courageous children have helped to rid the high seas of pirates."

The crowd waved their little flags.

Perry Pleaser continued, his teeth sparkling, "I hope all of you will vote for me in the next election."

Captain Sparkletooth took a step forward. "Prime Minister, is there any chance that you have a twin brother and that the two of you were separated at birth?"

"Why, yes," said the prime minister. "It is true."

"Is it also true that you love to look at yourself in the mirror and have your photograph taken?"

"Well, yes, that's true also."

"I knew it! I saw the resemblance immediately. You are my long-lost brother!"

The two men threw their arms around each other and had a good cry. Then they made plans to spend the entire evening together, discussing hair tonic and skin moisturizer and admiring each other's mirror collections.

Jacob Two-Two had to say good-bye to Cindy. They promised to telephone each other, and Jacob scratched Treasure behind the ears. Then Cindy and her mother stepped into a waiting limousine and sped away.

Jacob and his family crowded into a taxicab. They drove through the narrow streets of Montreal, past apartments with iron fire escapes zigzagging up their fronts. "At last I'm home again," said Jacob's father. "Let's stop at a delicatessen and get something to eat."

"I've just thought of something," Jacob's mother said. "We've been so busy that we haven't given Jacob a present for his birthday."

"That's right," said his father. "And if you ever deserved one, you do this year. What would you like, Jacob?"

Jacob thought for a moment. "I would like a pet. I've never had one. I've never had one."

"Alright," said his father. "We give in. What sort of pet do you want? A goldfish? A lizard? A cat or dog?"

"I don't know. Something different. Something different."

"We'll just have to find something, then," his father said with a smile. The cab bounced in and out of a pothole. Jacob looked out of the window at his new city. He hadn't been glad to leave his old home, but now he was looking forward to a new adventure. Jacob began to sing.

It's a brand-new life for us, hey ho!
A brand-new life for us!

And before he knew it, his whole family had joined in.

Other books in the *Jacob Two-Two* series:

Jacob Two-Two Meets the Hooded Fang
By Mordecai Richler, illustrated by Dušan Petričić

Poor Jacob Two-Two, only two plus two plus two years old and already a prisoner of The Hooded Fang. What had he done to deserve such terrible punishment? Why, the worst crime of all – insulting a grown-up.

Jacob Two-Two and the Dinosaur
By Mordecai Richler, illustrated by Dušan Petričić

When his parents bring a little green lizard home from their vacation in Kenya, Jacob Two-Two is thrilled. But as the days pass, he realizes that Dippy isn't an ordinary lizard. In fact, Dippy's not so little either. As Dippy grows bigger and bigger, he begins to attract attention from some very important people. Before Jacob realizes, he is on the run from the entire government!

Jacob Two-Two's First Spy Case
By Mordecai Richler, illustrated by Dušan Petričić

Just as Jacob Two-Two settles into his new life in Canada, things are turned upside down! First, Jacob gets a new neighbor, who does double duty as a spy; then his school gets a new principal, who turns out to be mean and nasty; and then, unknowingly, he makes an enemy – who could it be? Jacob Two-Two's adventure takes him into the fascinating world of spies.

Praise for Mordecai Richler's Jacob Two-Two series:

Jacob Two-Two Meets the Hooded Fang

"Mordecai Richler is a funny man, a good writer, and everyone should go out tomorrow morning and beat his local bookseller into submission if he hasn't got a nice plump display of books titled *Jacob Two-Two Meets the Hooded Fang*.... It is ghastly and funny... an unbelievably believable unbelievable place with no artificial sweeteners or preservatives."

— *The New York Times Book Review*

Jacob Two-Two and the Dinosaur

"The range and bite of this novel's hilarity will come as no surprise to fans of Mordecai Richler's adult fiction and of his previous book for children....Yet what's astonishing is how much of the humor here strikes both adult and child as genuinely funny." — *The New York Times Book Review*

"There is a reckless momentum to Richler's narrative, a rhythm of slap-dash invention that mimics the frantic pace of childhood fantasy. Yet Richler's tale is well-ventilated with adult wit."

— *Maclean's*

Jacob Two-Two's First Spy Case

"...the story combines zippy dialogue, clever magic tricks, and even a chapter in mirror writing, with opprobrious names and grossness galore.... It will undoubtedly be greeted with shrieks of joy and loud guffaws from children employing their all-too-natural baser instincts." — *The Horn Book Magazine*

"The book's centerpiece is a terrific little mind-reading swindle that Jacob and Mr. Dinglebat pull.... Readers will be baffled by the sophisticated scam, and delighted to find an appendix that teaches them how to replicate it.... [This book] is good silly fun..." — *The New York Times Book Review*